For Ivy —S.W.

For my sweets, Toddy and Doodles —M.G.

First Edition
1 3 5 7 9 10 8 6 4 2
H106-9555-5-13032
Printed in Malaysia • The art was created in pastel • Designed by Joann Hill
Library of Congress Cataloging-in-Publication Data
Watson, Stephanie Elaine, 1979–
The Wee Hours / by Stephanie Watson ; illustrated by Mary GrandPré.—First edition.
pages   cm
Summary: "A child's dreams take the form of mischievous Wee Hours who ransack her bedroom
until the milder morning hours come and put the Wee Hours to bed"—Provided by publisher.
ISBN 978-1-4231-4038-2—ISBN 1-4231-4038-9
[1. Dreams—Fiction. 2. Sleep—Fiction. 3. Bedtime—Fiction.] I. GrandPré, Mary, illustrator. II. Title.
PZ7.W3295We 2013   [E]—dc23   2012032397
Reinforced binding
Visit www.disneyhyperionbooks.com

The Wee Hours

BY Stephanie Watson   ILLUSTRATED BY Mary GrandPré

Disney • HYPERION BOOKS

NEW YORK

Late, late, late,
while you dreamed of a sunny Saturday,

the Wee Hours arrived.

The clock struck **one.**

The first Wee Hour pulled books from your shelf and read them upside down.

He built a tower from your shoes and knocked it flat.

He played his belly like a drum and sang, **Ba Ba Bo Bo Boo.**

He grabbed the sun from your dream and bounced it high like a ball.

While you dreamed of beautiful birds, the clock struck **two**.

The second Wee Hour emptied your closet and drawers, searching for a red sock to wear like a wig.

She did a happy dance in party tights.

She let the birds loose from your dream and taught them fancy tricks.

She put on a spellbinding play from behind your curtains.

While you dreamed of high-jumping horses, the clock struck **three**.

The third Wee Hour did one quick cartwheel, then another.

He swung from your ceiling fan and did backflips off your bedposts.

He freed the horses and led a jumping contest. The winners got prizes.

While you dreamed of a dozen dinosaurs, the clock struck **four**.

The fourth Wee Hour twirled like a tornado and sang,

Parade Time   Parade Time.

She pulled down your curtains
and waved them like flags.

She released the dinosaurs from your dream,
which made the birds flap and the horses race.

The Wee Hours laughed
    and cheered
        and marched and . . .

clapped and twirled

and skipped and · · ·

flipped and

leaped and . . .

The clock struck **five**.

Five O'Clock made a fort from your curtains and told everyone to gather close.

He whispered stories until the animals and the Wee Hours grew sleepy.

The clock struck **six**.

Six O'Clock led the sleepy animals back into your dreams.

She hung the curtains on the windows and picked up your toys and books.

The clock struck **seven**.

Seven O'Clock gathered fallen bird feathers
and tucked your shoes and socks away.

He smoothed your covers and
straightened your chairs.

Gently, gently, Five, Six, and Seven O'Clock
carried the Wee Hours off to bed.

They sang them songs and rubbed their backs
until the Wee Hours were fast asleep . . .

and dreaming of you.

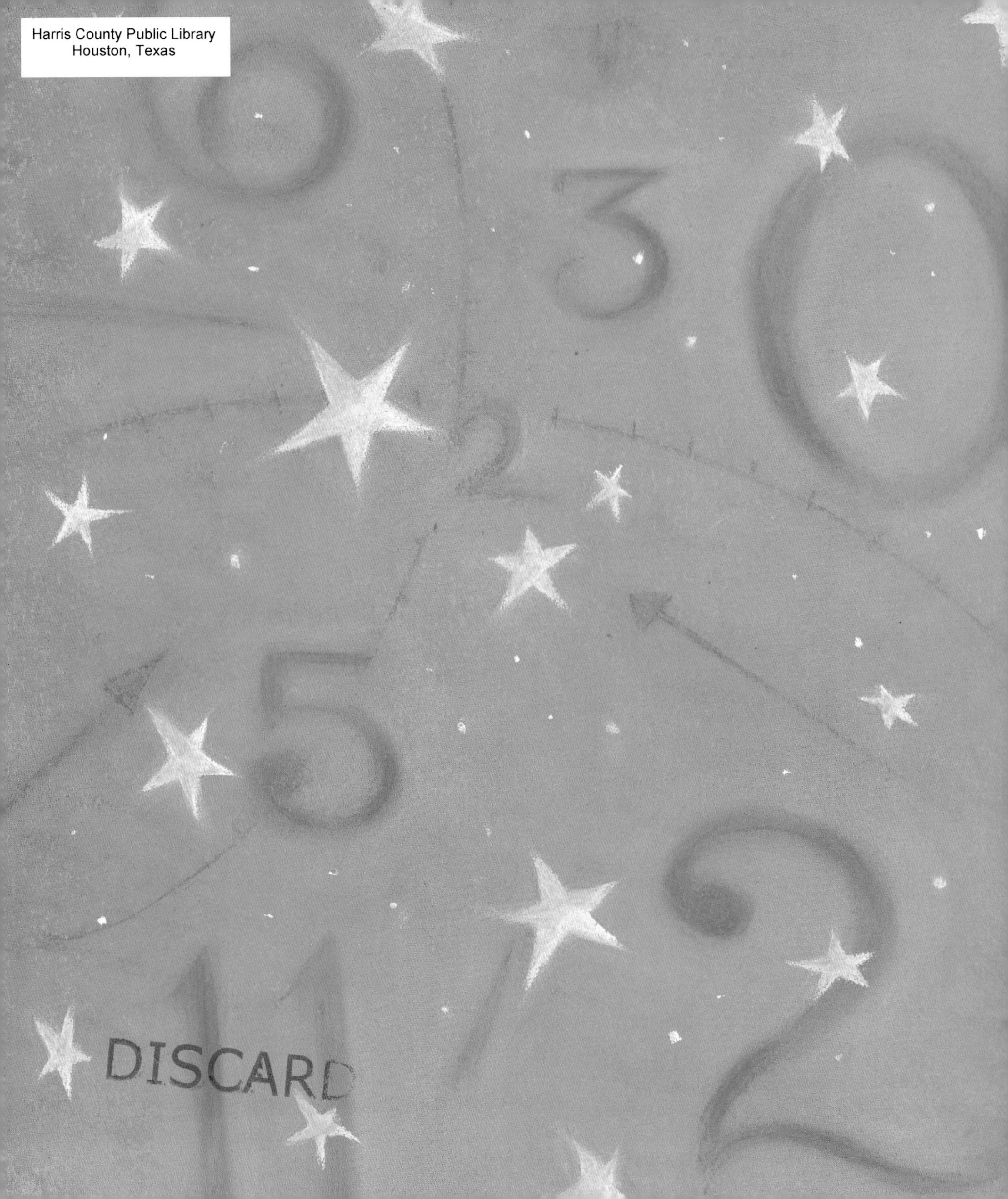